Endorsements for
Jazzy's Quest: What Matters Most

"*Jazzy's Quest: What Matters Most* covers adoption, history, and honesty in a way that is both engaging and accessible to early gradeschoolers. Carrie Goldman and Juliet Bond have come up with a story that will both entertain and open a doorway into some important conversations with your kiddos!"

– Addison Cooper, *Adoption at the Movies*

"*Jazzy's Quest* is an awesome book! I love how much it relates to my life! I was 9 when I read it, am Honduran-American, and was adopted as a baby by my parents who are not Hispanic."

– Bella, age 10

"Love this! *Jazzy's Quest: What Matters Most* is an engaging story that addresses for young readers friendship issues, diversity, inclusion, and more in such a sensitive and compassionate way."

– Trudy Ludwig
Bestselling author of *The Invisible Boy*
and *Confessions of a Former Bully*

The second installment of the *Jazzy's Quest* series is a complete and full story that will have you will compel you to keep reading until the very last page. While this is a book for elementary school aged readers, kids and adults alike will be able to glean a better understanding of what it is like to be a foster or adopted child from this tale. However, Carrie Goldman & Juliet Bond are able to weave a story in such a way that the reader is educated about the life and emotions of a foster/adoptive child without sacrificing a top-notch storyline. In addition caregivers will be very pleased to know that while the book highlights certain foster care and adoption issues, there is almost a 'normalizing' effect as other adoptees and foster children can see that other people have come up against similar issues as themselves. This book is a must for parents, caregivers, teachers, or anyone that would like their child to better empathize with others.

– Darren Fink, *Transfiguring Adoption*

"Is there any greater dilemma for a tween girl than deciding whether to stand with and up for your friends who are not included in the popular clique, or whether to grab a rare opportunity to join the popular kids when one arises? What happens when the decision to accept a birthday party invitation from the most popular girl in class has the potential to hurt a good friend who has been left out? This is the problem facing our heroine, Jazzy Armstrong, in the second early chapter book of the *Jazzy's Quest* series. 'What matters most' for Jazzy is at the heart of this book about friendship, social striving, and exclusionary behavior in elementary school. Jazzy learns that even through mistakes — or perhaps especially through mistakes — there can be redemption, and a deeper understanding of what it means to be a friend. In her quest to resolve her dilemma, Jazzy shows the reader the beauty and complexity of friendship, as well as the empathy and introspection it takes to grow up into a kind and principled human being."

– Lori Day, author of *Her Next Chapter: How Mother-Daughter Book Clubs Can Help Navigate Malicious Media, Risky Relationships, Girl Gossip, and So Much More*

Jazzy's Quest: What Matters Most
by Juliet C. Bond, LCSW & Carrie Goldman
Illustrated by Jeff Weigel

Printed in the United States of America.
Published by Marcinson Press, Jacksonville, Florida
© Copyright 2016 by Juliet Bond, LCSW & Carrie Goldman

ISBN 978-0-9967207-4-8

Published by
Marcinson Press
10950-60 San Jose Blvd., Suite 136
Jacksonville, FL 32223 USA
http://www.marcinsonpress.com

Jazzy's QUEST

WHAT MATTERS MOST

This book is dedicated to
some of the people who
MATTER MOST to us:

Kevin, Andrew, Jacob,
Mairita, Lilly, Toms, Katie,
Casey, Annie Rose,
Tomass, and Cleo.

TABLE OF CONTENTS

Dear Reader,

In fourth grade, finding the right friends
is one of the things that matters most. For
Jazzy and her new friend Michael, knowing
what matters most becomes difficult when
only one of them is invited to an exciting,
upcoming birthday party. If it were you,
would you choose the party or would you put
your friendship first?

Making friends is especially important for
Michael, who has been moved from foster
home to foster home, never really being able
to hang onto friendships. Now, he is finally
living with his forever family. Will Jazzy be
his first forever friend?

As friends ourselves, we know that there are
times when hard choices have to be made,
feelings get hurt, or friends need help.

We hope you enjoy reading the second
book in the *Jazzy's Quest* series, a story
about the complexities of friendship and the
importance of doing what matters most.

Warmly,
Juliet and Carrie

Chapter One
Hot Chocolate

Kids streamed around Jazzy Armstrong like schools of eager fish nudging one another as they poured through the double doors into the wintry air. "Hey!" Jazzy shivered as she leaned over her best friend Alec Waldon's wheelchair. "It's so cold – my mom might take us for hot chocolate today."

"She took us twice last week, Jazzy," Alec laughed. "I think we might be pushing our luck." He craned his neck to see a long line of cars snaking up the block. A bitter wind rushed past them as they stood by the curb.

"Pushing my luck is my specialty," she said, pulling her coat tight around her shoulders.

"Oh, I know. We've had rivers of hot chocolate this winter."

"And mountains of whipped cream," Jazzy sighed.

"But I can't go today," Alec said. "I have my first horseback riding class."

"Oh, right."

Alec had told her that his parents enrolled him in a special six-week horseback riding class. His doctor said it could help Alec build upper body strength for his favorite sport – wheelchair breakdancing. Alec had even won the most recent annual community talent show with his wheelchair breakdancing act.

"There's my mom!" Alec rolled forward as a car pulled towards the curb. Jazzy watched Alec's mom raise the wheelchair lift and load Alec into their blue minivan. "Bye!" Jazzy shouted as the door slid shut. But Alec didn't hear her.

The sidewalk near Jazzy's feet was crumbling in places. She dragged the toe of her gym shoe through a small pile of rubble and wondered what she might do after school now that Alec was busy. Turning, she overheard Shanice Tanner and Haley Smith talking.

"What are you going to do for your birthday party this year?" Shanice asked. Every January, Haley had incredible birthday parties. Well, at least, that was what Jazzy had heard.

"Will it be anything like the skate park party when you turned eight? That was amazing!" Shanice said. Her thick, black braids hung in pretty curls of colored ribbons. "I was so jealous that Lan Liu won the skateboard that year."

"It won't be anything like that year." Haley's eyes glittered.

Jazzy wished her mom would arrive. She bit her bottom lip, as she tried not to look like she was eavesdropping on Haley and Shanice.

"This year is going to be way better," Haley added.

Though they'd been in school together since kindergarten, Haley had never invited Jazzy to one of her birthday blowouts.

Shanice let out a tiny squeal. "Better than the Hawaiian beach blast you had last year? Oh my gosh, the s'mores were sooooo good! And the hula hoop contest!"

"And you did win the prize last year," Haley said.

"The iPod loaded with all of the songs the live band played! Boybands are so cool!"

A blue minivan waited next in line. Jazzy sighed and peered at the girls.

Haley dropped her voice and said, "This year, you're going to freak out at the prize, Shanice. I'll tell you, but you have to keep it secret." The girls' heads were so close that Shanice's dark braids wove themselves into Haley's blonde wisps.

"You know how my dad produces TV shows and movies?" Haley asked. Shanice nodded. "There's a little theater that my dad gets to use for press screenings and preview parties. This year, we're having a private screening of the new *Star Wars* movie at the theater!"

"Oh my gosh!" Shanice squealed.

Jazzy could swear she felt her heart melt into her purple gym shoes.

"Not only that," Haley went on, "all of my guests need to come in costume, because the best costume wins the prize!"

"What's the prize?" Shanice clung to Haley's arm.

Finally, Jazzy's red car pulled forward in the long line of parents picking up their kids. Jazzy strained to hear the rest of the girls' conversation.

"You can't tell anyone," Haley warned Shanice. "The winner of the costume contest gets to meet the *Star Wars* cast when they come to Chicago in March for C2E2, the biggest comic convention in Chicago!"

"No way!" Shanice yelled, her braids swinging. "I would, like, faint if I got to meet John Boyega! Finn is my favorite character in *The Force Awakens*!"

As Jazzy climbed into her mom's car, she heard Haley say, "Right? He's so cute!"

Wow! Haley's party sounded like Jazzy's dream come true, especially since it included a costume contest. Jazzy had a special talent for sewing costumes.

"But Haley would never invite me," she mumbled to herself.

"What's that?" Mom asked, looking over her shoulder. She turned back to the road, pushing up the bobby pin that held a clump of red curls. Both of Jazzy's older sisters, May and Sophie, also had red hair. Jazzy was the only one in the family with thick black curls and brown skin. Sometimes Jazzy really liked being the only adopted kid in her family, but other times, it was hard feeling different.

"Nothing," Jazzy said. She tugged down the zipper on her coat.

Mom turned the steering wheel to the left, pulling into traffic. "You seem like you're feeling down."

"It's no big deal," sighed Jazzy. "It's just that Alec is going to be really busy with his new riding class, so I basically have no friends. Plus, Haley Smith is having the most amazing birthday party ever this year, and there's no way she's inviting me. I'm just not popular."

"Oh, Jazzy," Mom said, reaching a hand backwards to squeeze Jazzy's knee. "Popularity isn't everything."

The sun shone through the front window, and

Jazzy shaded her eyes. "Well, it sure seems like the popular kids have more fun."

"Yeah, sometimes it can feel that way," Mom agreed.

"Mmmm," Jazzy replied. She was thinking about that party and the chance to make a new costume or meet an actor from the *Star Wars* films. She was also thinking about Alec. She missed their afternoons together already. As the treetops sped by outside the car window, Jazzy pictured the Alec-less, hot chocolate-less afternoons that lay ahead.

Chapter Two
Finding a Friend

The bell trilled just after Jazzy scooted into her seat. In front of the classroom, a lanky boy stood with his hands jammed into the pockets of his jeans. He wore a bright red shirt and bit the inside of his cheek as he scanned the faces of twenty-one fourth-graders looking back at him.

Ms. Weir's scratchy, cheerful voice filled the room. "Everybody, I would like to introduce you to Michael Larson. Michael moved here from North Carolina last month."

Alec tapped Jazzy's shoulder from behind, but she was too focused on the new boy's familiar features to notice.

"Michael is from the East Coast, so he is seeing his first Chicago snowstorm today!" Mrs. Weir said.

Jazzy caught her breath as she realized where she'd seen Michael before! He was the boy she'd met at the end of the community talent show. During their quick introduction, Jazzy had learned that Michael was recently adopted from foster care, loved *Star Wars* and, like Jazzy, had brown skin and a white adoptive family. Jazzy waved her hand to catch his attention. Michael stared at her for a beat.

"Hi," he mouthed. A wide smile of recognition spread all the way to his brown eyes.

Ms. Weir handed Michael a glossy math textbook and pointed toward an empty desk. Folding his long limbs into the chair, he flipped open the book.

"Okay, time to start learning!" said Ms. Weir. "What are the qualities of an equilateral triangle?"

Class seemed to go on forever. Afterwards, Jazzy looked for Michael. She was glad that it was time for recess so she and Michael could talk.

"Michael, over here!"

"Hi!" He rushed towards her. "I can't believe we're in the same school. Sweet!"

Alec wheeled his way towards them, already wearing his bulky winter coat.

"Michael, this is Alec, my best friend," Jazzy said. "We've known each other since we were five." She pulled the handle of her locker, and the door opened with a rusty squeak.

"Actually, Jazzy, we met when *I* was five," Alec teased. "You were still four and three quarters." Alec wheeled in a circle around her.

"Hey, I remember you!" Michael exclaimed. "You did that wheelchair breakdance number in the talent show. You were amazing! I still can't figure out how you did a handstand."

"Handstands are easy," replied Alec. "It's standing on my feet that gives me problems."

He laughed, and Michael joined in.

Jazzy pulled on her thick winter hat and favorite gloves.

With a confident stride, Haley approached

the group. "Alec can do all kinds of impressive things." She gave Alec a high five.

Ever since Alec won the community talent show, Haley had been super nice to him. Before that, she used to make comments about his wheelchair, but now she acted like they were best friends. Jazzy was happy that Haley wasn't making fun of Alec anymore. But it bugged Jazzy that Haley only took an interest in Alec *after* he became popular. To Jazzy, Alec had always been awesome.

"Alec, did you get the invitation to my party?" Haley asked.

Jazzy's eyes widened.

"You're coming, right?" Haley persisted. "I know how much you love *Star Wars*."

Alec looked at Jazzy. A pained expression flitted across his face. He mumbled, "Yeah, I'm going to your party. Thanks for the invitation."

Haley spotted Greta Williams. "Okay, I gotta get my coat for recess. See ya." She hurried off to catch up with Greta.

An awkward silence settled over the group.

"Were you also invited to her party?"

Michael asked Jazzy.

"No," she said. "I, um, I've never gone to one of her parties." Jazzy was afraid to meet Alec's gaze. They had always talked about how much they wanted to go to one of Haley's parties.

"I've missed a lot of birthday parties, too," Michael said softly. His eyes were kind. "When I was in foster care, I moved around a lot. I was always the new kid in school. Every time I started to make friends, I was placed in a new home and had to start over. No one ever knew me well enough to invite me to a birthday party."

Jazzy's stomach did a little twist. Maybe it was selfish to care about Haley's party.

"Is that why you moved here?" Alec asked. "To live with a new family?" He ripped open a bag of fruit gummies, offering Michael and Jazzy each a handful. Jazzy and Alec waited as Michael pulled his coat from his locker.

"Yeah, but this time it's permanent. I got adopted. So, it's, like, forever." Michael thrust one long arm into the sleeve of his coat.

"Like me," Jazzy said.

The three kids polished off the fruit gummies as they bundled up for recess. When Jazzy opened the door to the playground, a blast of frigid air whipped her curls back.

Alec struggled to navigate his wheelchair through the thick snow. Trying to help, Jazzy pushed, but the chair only moved a few inches before sliding sideways. Michael rushed to Alec's side and righted the chair.

"Hey, it's no big deal," Alec shrugged. "The chair won't move in this snow."

Jazzy frowned. "Aren't they supposed to have the exit shoveled for you?"

"Sometimes they shovel it in the morning, but the snow comes back so fast that it's too much of a slushy mess for my chair." Jazzy and her friends stopped in the doorway.

"I actually need to catch up on some studying. I'm so busy after school with my riding lessons; it's hard to find time to do homework. You go ahead." Alec backed into the building.

Jazzy wasn't sure about leaving Alec. She asked, "Do you want us to ask Ms. Weir if we can get a pass to go to the library with you?"

"Nah," Alec shook his head. He spun his chair to roll in the opposite direction.

Michael frowned. "Does that happen a lot?"

"Well," Jazzy said, "today is extra snowy. But it does happen sometimes."

"Maybe we should ask Ms. Weir about it," Michael said. "Alec shouldn't have to stay inside while everyone else gets to play."

"Yeah, let's definitely talk to Ms. Weir."

The kids walked towards a hill of snow on the playing field.

"Do you want to build a snowman?" Jazzy asked.

"How about a Snow Yoda?" Michael suggested.

"Yeah! And we can use a stick for his lightsaber!" They goofed around, molding the wet snow into the shape of Yoda's body. Michael struck a pose next to Yoda. "Take a pic of me with Snowda!" Jazzy pretended to click a camera.

"So," Michael said, "I heard Ms. Weir call you Jasmine, but Alec called you Jazzy. Which name do you go by?"

"Both," Jazzy laughed. "Teachers almost always call me Jasmine, but my family and my good friends call me Jazzy." She hesitated and then added, "So you can call me Jazzy, okay?"

"Sweet!" Michael said. Jazzy threw a snowball at him. It crushed in a star-shaped splotch against his navy blue coat. "Oh, you're going to regret that," he laughed.

Jazzy grabbed another handful of snow. "Hey, do you want to come over after school? I still haven't seen Monday's episode of *Star Wars Rebels*, and it's on our DVR," she said.

"Let me ask my mom when she comes to pick me up. But I'm pretty sure she'll say yes. She was nervous this morning, hoping I'd make a friend. Wait till she hears that you go to this school! I bet she'll remember you from the talent show." Michael propped a crooked stick into the Snowda's hand. "Done!" he said. Then, in a perfect Yoda voice, Michael squawked, "Amazing you will be!"

Jazzy fell into the snow, laughing.

Chapter Three

Rebels

"Scoot over, chicken nuggets," Dad joked. "Make room for Luke Sock-walker!" Kernels of popcorn spilled from a large, yellow bowl balanced on his lap.

"Da-aad." Jazzy grinned at Michael. "My dad always wears his lucky *Star Wars* socks when we watch the show," she explained.

"Sweet socks, Mr. Armstrong. You might be my favorite new person."

Pulling up the cuff of his pants, Michael flashed his own pair of blue and white R2D2 socks.

"Whoaaa! What's up, sock twin?" Slapping

a high five with Michael, Dad said, "You are most definitely my favorite new person!" Dad fumbled with the remote control. Jazzy took it from him, and within seconds, the opening theme music of *Star Wars Rebels* soared from the TV. Michael grabbed a handful of popcorn. "My dad gets all emotional every time the opening music starts to play."

Jazzy shook her head. "Mine too. Geez, get it together, dads."

Jazzy's dad held firm. "Hey, dads have sensitive souls."

"Then how come you never cry at the sad puppy commercials, huh?" Jazzy challenged.

"Puppies scare me." Dad pulled a blanket over his head.

Jazzy groaned at her dad's corny joke as a commercial caught her interest.

An important announcement from WGN-TV! Lucasfilm is hosting an Art and Design contest in Chicago for kids ages 6-12. Enter your own one-of-a-kind creation for a chance to win an all-expenses-paid trip for your family to Skywalker Ranch! Go to www.starwars.com

for more details on how to register for the big competition, which will be held at McCormick Place on Saturday, March 18th! May The Force Be With You!

With her mouth full, Jazzy said, "Wait! Dad, pause the show."

Michael pointed at the television. "We have to go look that up!"

"Yes. We have to," Jazzy said. Jazzy's dad held his palms in the air.

"I guess if we have to…" he chuckled. Jazzy's dad hopped off the couch, racing to beat the kids to the den.

Jazzy and Michael laughed as they followed him. Michael's long fingers skittered across the keyboard typing in the web address. Dad leaned in, squinting at the tiny font. "Where did I put my eyes?" he asked.

Michael furrowed his brow at Jazzy in confusion.

"My dad always loses his glasses," Jazzy explained.

"The kitchen? Or maybe in the living room?" Dad wondered. "I'll be right back," he said, leaving the office to rummage through the house.

Michael and Jazzy scrolled down the web page. "Look!" Michael pointed out. "It says kids can dress in costumes. What will you wear? That Cloud City Leia cape you made for the talent show?"

"I don't know." Jazzy scrunched her eyebrows. "Maybe I should make something new from *The Force Awakens*. Hey, I know! I could make Rey's costume as my entry into the contest!"

Jazzy looked at Michael. "Do you have a costume to wear?"

"No, not really." Michael paused as if he were deciding whether or not to tell Jazzy something important. He took a deep breath. "In my last foster home – before my parents adopted me – I had this authentic Chewbacca mask. But every time I got moved, I was only allowed to bring whatever I could fit into a plastic garbage bag, so I had to leave it behind."

"That's awful," Jazzy said.

"Yeah."

Jazzy thought about all of her things. In her room, the bookshelves sagged, heavy with the weight of all the books and toys her parents had bought her over the years. She wished Michael had been able to keep everything that mattered to him.

Jazzy clapped her hands. "Michael, let's enter the contest as a team and make something together!"

"That would be great! But I can't sew."

"It doesn't have to be a costume. You know what would be so cool?"

Michael waited as Jazzy leaned in and grabbed his arm. "Let's make a model of Rey's speeder, the one she built from scavenged parts."

Michael spun in the desk chair, his knobby knees banging into a drawer. "Yes! I can help you with that. My mom's lab has a gigantic 3D printer."

"And then we can paint it and attach accessories to make it look exactly like the real one!"

Filling out the online registration form, Michael asked, "Whose address should we put down for prize notification? Yours?"

"Sure. I'll type it in. Oh, and look! The winner also gets a cash prize of $200. We could split that."

"Sweet," Michael said.

When Michael's mom came to pick him up that night, he ran to the door.

"Jazzy and I are going to enter a *Star Wars* Art and Design contest. We might even win a trip to Skywalker Ranch, but we need to use your professional 3D printer."

Michael's mom laughed. "Well, this all sounds exciting!" She turned to Jazzy's dad.

He ran his fingers through his thinning hair. "I guess we'd better get used to being the parents of famous prizewinners. What do you wear to a press conference?"

The hallway felt electric with excitement. "Wait!" Jazzy called out, as Michael stepped outside. "You forgot your backpack." The kids ran off, leaving the adults standing at the door.

Michael's mom shook her head. "This

is the happiest I've seen Michael since we brought him home. Thank you for sharing your daughter and your love of *Star Wars* with him."

"We should be thanking you," Jazzy's dad said. "Jazzy's had a lot more questions about being adopted as she's gotten older. We really started noticing it when she turned ten. Having a friend who was also adopted is really good for her."

The kids tumbled back into the hallway.

"So we need to come to your lab tomorrow," Michael told his mom. "We have to get started with the images right away, because you told me that it takes a few days to print big things on the 3D printer. The contest is in two weeks."

"Slow down," Michael's mom said. "You're moving at light speed." She smiled at Jazzy's dad.

"I can get Jazzy to your lab after her appointment tomorrow." Dad always called Antonia's phone calls "appointments" in case Jazzy didn't want to go into a whole explanation about her open adoption.

Jazzy explained, "My appointment is

actually a phone call. My birth mom, Antonia, calls once a month. And I get to talk to my birth brother too. His name is Carlos. He's seven. He gave me this wristband from his soccer team." She held out her wrist, displaying the orange rubber WILDKITS bracelet that she wore everywhere.

"Oh," Michael's smile faltered. "That's fine."

"What's wrong?" Jazzy asked.

Michael glanced at his mom, who was helping Jazzy's dad enter the address of her office into his phone. "Nothing, I'm good."

Wondering if Michael didn't want to talk about something in front of his mom, Jazzy decided to ask him about his birth family later, when they were alone.

"What time do you think you will get to the lab, Jazzy?" Michael asked. "It's at Northwestern University on Sheridan Road. Mom, tell them the address of your office."

"I've got the coordinates punched into the Falcon's nav system." Jazzy's dad held up his phone. "Standby for blast off!"

"I'll be there by 10:30," Jazzy said.

"G'night, Jazzy!" Michael waved as he walked down the porch steps with his mom.

Jazzy waved back. "May the Force be with you!" she called.

Chapter Four
Late Arrival

The next day, sun blazed across the snow. Jazzy noticed slippery areas of water forming on top of thick slabs of ice in her driveway as she peered out of the living room window. Dad tossed a green apple to Jazzy.

"Ready?" he asked.

"Mmm, hmm," Jazzy answered. She slipped the cool apple into the pocket of her sweatshirt.

Dad handed Jazzy his phone. Antonia picked up after the first ring. "Hi, Jasmine!" Her voice was light and musical.

"Hi," Jazzy answered. "How are you?"

"We're doing great," Antonia said. "We

miss you! The yearly summer picnic can't come fast enough." Jazzy's birth family and her adoptive family got together two times a year, once for a picnic in the summer and once for a holiday dinner in December. This was part of their open adoption agreement.

"I miss you, too," Jazzy said. "Is Carlos there?" In some ways, the hardest part about being in an open adoption was that Jazzy didn't get to see her birth brother, Carlos, as much as she'd like. Carlos was funny, smart, and looked just like Jazzy. "Sure, he's right here."

"Hey, Carlos. How's your soccer team doing this year?"

"Great!" he said. "We won the playoffs."

"Wow! That's fantastic!"

Jazzy doodled on a notepad as she chatted with Carlos about the big game. By the time Jazzy got off the phone, it was almost 10:30 am. She was going to be late to meet Michael.

"Carlos, I have to go meet a friend."

Carlos moaned, "But I want to tell you about my science project!"

"Okay, yeah. Tell me."

He described every detail of his project. Jazzy began to worry about being late to meet Michael, but she didn't want to end her conversation with Carlos. Finally, Carlos said goodbye.

"I love you, Jazzy."

"I love you more," Jazzy said. She blew a loud squeaky kiss into the phone. Carlos giggled. It always made Jazzy feel warm inside when Carlos laughed, especially when she was the one who made him happy.

It was now 10:35 a.m., and Jazzy was officially late to meet Michael. She grabbed her backpack and called out, "Dad, I'm ready to go!" Stooping down to nuzzle her dog Sing, Jazzy waited. Dad poked his head out of the living room.

Dad had been listening to Jazzy's older sister Sophie practice her cello. Except for Jazzy, everyone in the family was musically gifted. They even had a family band called The Amazing Armstrongs. Jazzy liked music, but she was far more interested in sewing and designing costumes. It was one of the things that made her unique within her family.

The gentle sounds of Sophie playing Bach's Cello Suite No. 1 floated behind Dad as he walked towards Jazzy. "All right, kiddo, let's go." Dad grabbed his keys from the cluttered hall table. "Hey, my missing glasses! Hello, eyes," he said, slipping them on.

When Dad and Jazzy finally pulled up in front of the lab, Michael was pacing back and forth outside. Jazzy opened the car door and bounded towards Michael.

"Where were you?" he asked, jamming his hands deep in his pockets. "It's almost eleven. You said you would be here half an hour ago." He stared at the ground. Piles of dirty snow and chunks of ice littered the sidewalk. Behind him stood the massive white building where Michael's mother worked. It was so big that it reminded Jazzy of the Pentagon in Washington, D.C.

"I was talking to my little brother, Carlos. I lost track of time. He and I only catch up once a month. I'm sorry."

Michael's baseball cap was pulled low over

his brow. He held still for a moment. "I thought you weren't coming," he said quietly.

"I should have had my dad text your mom to say we were running behind."

Michael's jaw softened. He let out a heavy puff of air. "I guess it was just hard to believe you were going to show up. Usually, when people are late, it means they forgot about me. At least, that's how it's been."

Jazzy cocked her head, listening. She kicked a nugget of ice along the sidewalk toward Michael. He trapped it with his foot and then kicked it back toward her.

"I really am sorry I was late," Jazzy said. "I didn't mean for you to worry."

Michael took a deep breath. "I used to wait for my sister and my mom to show up for visits. After about fifteen minutes, I knew they weren't coming."

Jazzy tried to imagine what that felt like. "Do you ever see them anymore?" she asked.

"When I was little, my mom would come every now and then. But the visits grew further and further apart. Then she stopped showing up. By the time I was moved to my last foster home, we didn't even know where she was or how to reach her. I haven't seen her since I was six."

"What about your sister?" Jazzy said.

Michael hesitated. "She, umm, she has problems with anger and stuff. She lives in a special home for teens that get into trouble. I don't have any contact with her, either." He swallowed and sent the marble of ice skittering off the sidewalk and into the grass. Jazzy lunged after it and tapped it back to him.

Michael watched the little stone tumbling toward him and smiled. "But we did used to have fun together sometimes. My sister could make a game out of anything!"

"I bet you miss her," Jazzy said, twisting a spongy black curl around her finger.

"Yeah, I do. I really do."

"You know, Michael," Jazzy told him, "I kind of understand. I mean, it's not the same for me, because I do get to see my birth mom and Carlos during visits. But sometimes I feel sort of empty, like I'm homesick for something. I don't know how to explain it. Sometimes I feel like I don't fit in exactly — even with my own family."

Michael stared at Jazzy. "Yes! I know that feeling! I get that way, too."

"But then," Jazzy continued, "I go talk to my parents or my sisters, and it helps. We hang out and play a game or watch a movie, and after a while, I feel okay again. Can you talk to your parents?" She pushed another bouncy lock off her forehead.

Michael pointed toward the entrance of the building. Jazzy fell into step beside him, speeding up to keep up with his long legs.

"Yeah. I'm learning to talk about this stuff with my mom and dad," he said. "And you're right. It does feel better after a while, like my stomach isn't so tight." His face brightened. "Actually, I already feel better than I did when I was waiting for you."

"Good," Jazzy said. "So, will you show me the 3D printer in your mom's lab?"

"Yeah. Let's go inside. I'm freezing!"

Jazzy followed him up the stone steps and

leaned forward to pull open the heavy door.

"This building is a maze," said Michael. "The Northwestern students call it 'Tech' and their library is 'The Mother Ship.'" He and Jazzy walked down a winding hallway. College students milled around the doorways, clutching sheaths of paper.

Michael's mom was bent over a shiny silver microscope. She wore a crisp, white lab coat. Michael and Jazzy raced into the room.

"Hi, Jazzy!" Michael's mom said with a warm smile. "Is this the first time you've used a 3D printer?"

"Yep! But I read all about them last night on the Internet. And I already made four drawings of Rey's speeder, each from a different point of view," Jazzy said, holding up her sketchbook.

"Good idea," Michael said. "So we can make sure it looks right from all angles." The two kids settled in front of a computer, heads together, and began to work. Michael's mom studied them, her eyes shining.

Chapter Five

Rewriting History

The students watched as Ms. Weir unfolded pieces of white paper, reading them each aloud. During their history lesson, she'd asked them to write down the most important social action or event that happened in their lifetime.

"Okay, let's see what you all believe matters most! The first one is... the election of the first black president," Ms. Weir read.

The kids murmured in agreement. That was certainly an important historical event that had happened in Jazzy's lifetime.

Ms. Weir opened another. "My blowout birthday parties," she said. A few kids chuckled.

It was pretty obvious who wrote that one. Ms. Weir even looked at Haley. Jazzy clenched her fist around a pencil.

Ms. Weir opened another slip of paper and read, "The Christopher Reeves Act that gave rights to disabled people."

Jazzy turned to Michael. She whispered, "That reminds me. We need to talk to Ms. Weir about cleaning snow off the path so that Alec's wheelchair can get outside for recess."

Michael's chair screeched as he scooted forward a bit. "Yes, totally."

"We got a puppy!" Ms. Weir read. There was a collective "awwww" from the class. Jazzy remembered her dad's joke that he was afraid of puppies.

Ms. Weir paused. "Now, all of these events are important, right?"

The children nodded their heads as they looked around the room at each other.

"But people in power, like historians or politicians, get to decide what matters most and those are the only events that make the history books. So, since I'm the one in power in this classroom, I get to decide which event was the most important thing that happened in your lifetime."

She shuffled through the papers and pulled one out. The kids waited, their faces turned up with interest.

"I have decided that what matters most is that... Gordy McDaniel got a puppy!" Ms. Weir announced.

The students shifted in their seats. Alec frowned. Jazzy raised her hand, "But Ms. Weir, that's not fair. I mean, that may have been most important to Gordy, but..."

"I'm in charge," Ms. Weir said, depositing the remaining scraps of paper into the garbage. "I get to decide what is most important and what future generations will know about history."

"But what about the first black president?" Michael asked.

"Yeah, and disability rights?" Jazzy crossed her arms.

Alec adjusted his wheelchair.

"Nope," Ms. Weir smiled. "I think future

generations should concentrate on nice things like puppies."

Shaking her head, Jazzy spoke up again. "That's not right. One person alone shouldn't get to decide," she said.

Ms. Weir stepped over to Jazzy's desk. She tapped her chin with one finger. "It isn't right, is it, Jasmine? If only a few powerful people get to decide, a lot of important events and causes are lost to history." Turning toward the rest of the class, Ms. Weir asked, "How did you feel when I decided that your event wasn't important?"

"Like I didn't matter," Haley muttered.

Ms. Weir nodded. "That's exactly right. People of color, people without money or power — women, much of the time, — are mostly left out of history books, which makes them feel like they don't matter. So, your assignment is to go home, pick something that matters most to you, and show us all why your project might belong in a history book."

The bell rang and the kids filed out. Jazzy and Michael hung back.

"Ms. Weir?" Jazzy asked. "We have a cause

we want to talk to you about." She looked at Michael. "Um... it seems unfair that Alec can't always go outside during recess, because the snow doesn't get shoveled from the path to the playground."

"You're right. This is a perfect way to address the assignment. Why don't you two work on this one together? And I'll think about it too."

The kids made their way into the hallway, bubbling with determination.

"I like this school," Michael said. "We didn't talk about these kinds of things at my last school."

"Yeah, I never thought about the way some history gets lost," Jazzy said.

Michael shrugged, "I think about it all the time. I hardly know any of my own history. Like, I have no idea who my biological dad is, and the social workers don't tell me anything."

"You don't have any idea?" Jazzy asked.

"I asked my grandma when she was still alive, but she just said she would tell me when I was older."

"That's unfair, too."

"Yeah." Michael wound the string of his hoodie around his thin fingers. "But we should figure out what to do about the snow blocking the sidewalk, right?"

"Let's talk to Mr. Budzik, the janitor, after school. He must be in charge of shoveling the walks, right?"

"Great idea!"

At 3:35 p.m., Jazzy and Michael found Mr. Budzik lifting chairs and placing them upside down on top of the long tables in the cafeteria.

"Mr. Budzik?" Jazzy started.

Her turned, his wide arms holding a chair by its legs.

"Can we ask you about the sidewalk?" Michael asked.

Mr. Budzik leaned closer. "Ya?"

"Our friend Alec Waldon uses a wheelchair. Sometimes Alec can't get out to play during recess... when the snow isn't shoveled."

"Ah," Mr. Budzik said. "I try to get this done, but I also have to shovel the main door, because the lunch deliveries arrive at the same time."

54

"Isn't there anyone else who can do it?" Michael asked.

"It's just me," Mr. Budzik said, rubbing his chin.

Jazzy's shoulders drooped. "Ok, thanks."

Mr. Budzik had soft wrinkles around his eyes that grew deeper as he looked at Jazzy and Michael. "I'm very sorry."

The kids made their way out to the front of the school. "We'll have to think of something else," Michael said.

"Yeah, let's talk about it while we work on the speeder today." Turning her thoughts to the *Star Wars* Art and Design Competition, Jazzy followed Michael to his mom's waiting car. They'd arranged to go back to her lab to finish up their project. The final few pieces had finished printing, and Jazzy couldn't wait to see them. Rey's speeder was beginning to look so real that she could picture herself riding on it.

At dinner that night, Sophie kidded Jazzy, "When are you going to show us your speeder, Rey?"

"Soon!" said Jazzy. "It's all done, but

Michael's going to keep it at his house until the competition."

Sophie started to hum the *Star Wars* theme song. Sing, the dog, howled along. "Everybody's a joker in this family," Jazzy moaned.

"Huskies are known for their singing voices," Sophie said, nudging Jazzy.

"Sing is only part Husky. She's half sheepdog, too." It had always meant a lot to Jazzy that Sing was from two different families, just like she was.

Dad's phone vibrated just as the family finished dessert. He glanced at it and handed it to Jazzy. "For you," Dad said. "I'm just the social secretary around here."

Jazzy took the phone and headed into the living room. Sing padded along beside her. "Jazzy! You aren't going to believe it!" Alec sounded out of breath.

"I asked Haley if she would invite you to her birthday party, and she said yes! Can you believe it? You're going to meet the cast of *Star Wars* with me! Well, if we win the prize, that is!"

Jazzy couldn't help it. She squealed with joy. "Oh my gosh!" Sing's ears pricked up. "I might meet Daisy Ridley!"

"What are you going to wear?"

Jazzy thought about the Cloud City cape she'd worn at the community talent show. No, she needed something new. This would be her chance to sew a Rey costume, and then she could wear also it to the competition with Michael!

Thinking of the competition made Jazzy's stomach drop. "What about Michael?" Jazzy asked. "Do you think you could ask Haley if she'd invite Michael too?"

Alec hesitated. "Actually, I did ask her about Michael. She said that she couldn't add any more people."

"Oh, um," Jazzy said. "I understand. It was really nice of you to ask."

"Thanks. I wish he could come too. I know he likes *Star Wars* as much as you do. Anyway, the party starts at eleven next Saturday. My mom said she can drive us."

"Cool," Jazzy said. "I'm really excited!"

"Me too," Alec said.

As soon as they hung up, Jazzy realized that next Saturday was the same day as the *Star Wars* Art and Design Competition.

She sank onto the floor. Sing stared at her from the carpet.

"Oh, no," Jazzy groaned.

Jazzy drew Sing's heavy body close to hers. The thick strands of fur that covered Sing's body were surprisingly soft. Leaning back onto her side, Jazzy took a heavy breath. "I've wanted to go to Haley's parties since I was in first grade, Sing."

Sing thumped her tail. "What am I going to do?"

Chapter Six

The Lie

The next morning, Jazzy's toast stuck in her throat in dry clumps. During the car ride to school, she barely spoke.

"Mom, can you put this song on repeat?" Sophie asked. "Taylor Swift is my favorite."

"Not again!" groaned May. "We already heard this one twice in a row, right, Jazzy?"

Jazzy shrugged.

She dragged her feet during the long walk from the parking lot to the main entrance of the school. Inside the building, the air felt too hot. Jazzy unzipped her puffy jacket and stuffed it into her locker.

"Hi, Jazzy!" Michael appeared at her locker.

"Oh," Jazzy tried to smile. "Hey, Michael."

"You okay?" Michael asked. He unzipped his backpack and pulled out his red homework folder.

"I'm just tired," she whispered.

"Well, you're going to need to save your strength. I brought snow shovels from home. I thought we could ask Ms. Weir if we could leave class a little bit early to shovel the playground for Alec."

"Great idea," Jazzy said. "That was kind of you."

Jazzy had PE second period. She followed Haley, Shanice, and Greta into the locker room to change. The smell of Lysol and feet clung to the wooden benches. Haley almost let the door swing shut as Jazzy entered, but Haley paused to hold it open for Jazzy. She never did that.

"Did Alec tell you that you can come to my party, Jazzy?" Jazzy followed the three girls to a bench where they began changing into gym shoes.

"Yes," Jazzy said. "Thank you for inviting

me." Her fingers fumbled with the laces as she knotted her sneakers. The thought of Haley's party started a swarm of butterflies flapping inside her belly.

"Will you wear one of your *Star Wars* costumes?" Haley asked. "They are really mind blowing. I even told my dad about your collection."

"Really?" Jazzy's eyes widened.

"But you can't dress up as Rey," said Haley. "I'm going to be her."

Jazzy opened her mouth but then closed it again. If she couldn't go as Rey, maybe she would go as Padme Amidala. She had always wanted to make Padme's gorgeous parade gown.

"Which one is Rey?" asked Greta. "I know this is crazy, but I haven't seen the *Star Wars* movies."

"Rey is the scavenger who turns out to have hidden Jedi powers," explained Jazzy.

Her hands grew cold as she remembered how Michael was counting on her to go with him to the *Star Wars* Art and Design Competition.

"Come on, girls," bellowed Coach Zimmerman. "Today we see how many sit-ups you can do in a minute. Find a partner to hold your feet."

Haley touched Jazzy on the shoulder. "Do you want to be partners?"

Haley had never asked Jazzy before! Jazzy made her decision. She would go to the birthday party. She would just have to find a way to tell Michael without hurting his feelings.

Coach Zimmerman clapped her hands together three times. "Everyone, let's get a move on."

After gym class, Jazzy met Michael by the playground door. He handed her a shovel, and they began to scoop mounds of snow off the sidewalk. The weight of the snow dragged Jazzy's arms down, matching the heaviness she felt inside.

"Michael, there is something I have to tell you," she started. She couldn't meet his eyes.

"What? Is something wrong?" Michael asked. He hacked at a slab of ice blocking the sidewalk.

"I, uh, can't make it to the *Star Wars* Art and Design Competition on Saturday."

"What?" Michael froze in place. "Why not?"

"Sophie has a cello concert," Jazzy lied. "And it's really important, because it is the biggest concert of the year. She has a long solo."

Michael was silent. A gust of freezing wind stung Jazzy's cheeks.

"Umm..." Jazzy chewed her lip. "I'm really sorry, but Sophie's so nervous, and my parents said everyone has to be there to support her." Jazzy cringed. This was a dumb lie, even to Jazzy. Her parents would never really make her skip the *Star Wars* competition. They were as excited about it as she was.

"But didn't you already know the date of the concert?" Michael whispered.

Jazzy couldn't stop the lies. "Sophie wrote it down wrong."

There was a long pause as Michael drew in a shaky breath. "I guess you have to be there for your sister. I sure would want my sister to be there for me." Every word Michael said pierced

Jazzy's heart with guilt.

They worked without talking for the next few minutes. The only sound was the steady scraping of the shovels.

"I'm going to take my coat off," Michael said. Using his scarf, he wiped beads of sweat from his forehead. The hard work didn't warm Jazzy. Lying to Michael felt like frosty fingers running up her back.

When the recess bell rang, Michael looked across the playground. "We've only cleared the first part of sidewalk."

"This little bit took all of our time." Jazzy leaned onto her shovel.

The recess bell clanged. Kids tumbled out of the building, shouting and running. After the initial crowd squeezed through, the familiar sound of Alec's wheelchair scraped across the pavement.

Alec easily covered the first half of the sidewalk. When he reached the part they hadn't shoveled yet, his chair came to a sudden halt. Gripping the wheels, Alec leaned forward, determined to roll the wheelchair through the slippery snow. The chair rolled ahead a few inches and then lurched backwards. Alec looked at Jazzy and Michael. He gave a small shrug.

"Do you want us to push you?" Michael asked.

Alec brushed his wet gloves together, wiping away the clumps of muddy snow from the wheels of his chair. "It's okay, guys," Alec said. "We can hang out here. Really. Thanks for shoveling a path."

The three kids talked as if nothing were wrong. But Jazzy noticed how Alec kept looking at the basketball court, where Gordy McDaniel was shooting baskets. Alec loved to practice free throws during recess, but in the winter he often couldn't get through the snow to that section of the playground. The kids made awkward attempts at conversation.

Ms. Weir stopped Michael and Jazzy as they exited the playground. "Any luck on the project?" she asked.

The two friends shook their heads. "We'll think of something," Michael said.

Jazzy wasn't so sure.

Chapter Seven
Some Good Advice

For the rest of the afternoon, Ms. Weir's words were blurry, muffled sounds that floated past Jazzy. All she could think about was Haley's party. Jazzy had planned to tell Michael the truth, but it was too hard, too shameful, so she lied.

After school, she trudged toward the curb. What was she going to tell her parents? What was she going to do about Dad? He was expecting to drive Michael and her to the *Star Wars* Art and Design Competition and be with them all day. The remnants of her spaghetti lunch soured in her mouth.

Dad pulled up with May already in the car.

"Where's Sophie?" Jazzy asked.

"Sophie is having a sleepover at Daniella's house tonight."

Jazzy gulped. "Dad, Michael's mom wants to take us to the *Star Wars* competition on Saturday."

"Great! Why don't we all drive together?" Dad said.

"No," Jazzy shook her head. "No," she repeated. May turned and gave her a strange look.

"I, uh, wanted to bike over there. And I think it will be special for Michael's mom to do this with us. She is really excited about it."

Dad was quiet.

Jazzy held her breath.

"Well, okay, if that's what you want," Dad said. "I was kind of looking forward to being there."

"I know," Jazzy said, "but Michael's mom really wants to be the one."

In the rearview mirror, Jazzy could make out Dad's resigned smile. "Of course she does. I'll come to the next one."

Jazzy noticed that she was still holding her breath. Exhaling slowly, Jazzy stared at her hands. It was all arranged. Jazzy was going to Haley's amazing birthday party.

On Saturday morning, Jazzy dressed carefully. She pulled the gown on first. The fabric was a cream colored satin that Jazzy had found in the remnants room of her local craft store, Vogue Fabrics. She had embroidered a long panel that fit the front of the dress. Next, Jazzy drew the long shawl across her shoulders. For this piece, Jazzy had gathered layers of peach chiffon, creating a sort of feathery cape. Last, Jazzy attached a rainbow-shaped neckpiece to the back of the dress.

In the mirror, Jazzy looked sort of like the character. She squared her shoulders. That was better, but something didn't feel quite right. Maybe it was her hair or face?

Jazzy headed to Sophie and May's room for help with her makeup. As usual, May lay curled in her giant beanbag, watching YouTube videos on her phone. Piles of clothes covered most of the carpet, and paperback books were tumbled within the folds of her blue comforter.

"Wow!" May sat up as Jazzy entered the room. "You look amazing!"

"Thanks," Jazzy said. "Can you help with the hair and makeup?"

"No problem." May stood to collect the hairbrushes and various pots and tubes that she kept in a giant, plastic caddy. Ever since May turned fourteen and was allowed to wear makeup, she hoarded lipsticks and blushes in heaps across her room. Sophie, who had just turned twelve, thought that makeup was weird. She favored a dirty, old Chicago Bears hat and a series of T-shirts Dad used to wear in college. "Let's get started. I bet you are so excited about the competition!"

"Yeah," Jazzy said.

May rubbed white greasepaint into Jazzy's cheeks. Then she tilted her head sideways. "Why do you keep chewing your lip, Jazzy? You always do that when something's wrong."

Jazzy suddenly felt as though she couldn't tell one more lie. She wondered if May would understand why Jazzy needed to go to Haley's

party. "I lied," she whispered. "I'm not going to
the competition with Michael."

May's hands grew still. "But you're all
dressed up?"

"I know. I'm going to Haley Smith's birthday party. It's a costume party."

May was quiet.

"Every year, I have to hear about Haley's huge birthday parties, and I've never been invited! And now that she's friends with Alec because he's popular, he got her to invite me to her party. This one is going to be the best ever because it's a *Star Wars* party and Haley actually wants me to come. But it's at the same time as the competition with Michael." Jazzy gulped a huge breath of air. "And Haley's parties always have these unbelievable prizes, and this year the winner gets to go to C2E2 and meet the cast of *Star Wars*."

"Wait, so you lied to Michael?"

"Yeah." Jazzy's chin sunk forward.

"And Mom and Dad?"

"Everyone," Jazzy whispered.

May pulled Jazzy's hair back into a slick bun, pinning the rolls of dark hair into tight curls. "Jazzy, this party must be really important to you if you are missing the *Star Wars* competition and lying to people you love."

"I've never been invited, not once." Jazzy could feel the tears welling up, threatening to spill across the beautiful makeup that May had just applied. "Oh no, now I'm ruining the makeup!"

Grabbing a tissue, May dabbed at her sister's watery eyes. "I think you may be ruining more than just makeup. This could go all wrong." She sighed. "Remember a year ago when I took Sophie's new jacket and wore it without asking? I got that horrible chocolate stain on it at the spring concert, and I couldn't get it out. When I tried bleaching it, the spot turned white against the pretty blue."

Jazzy blinked at the memory. She'd seen May scrubbing at the jacket, rushing around frantically while she tried to find something that would take the stain out.

"Finally, I just hid the jacket."

Jazzy remembered how the jacket was found. "But Sing pulled it out of the back of the closet, because she smelled the chocolate still on it."

May groaned at the memory. "And she chewed a huge hole in it – making everything worse!"

"Mom found it on the kitchen floor," Jazzy laughed. "And Sing had a stomachache and spent the rest of the day sulking in her crate."

"I had to use all of my babysitting money to replace Sophie's jacket and also do her chores for a week. But the worst thing was that Sophie didn't trust me around her things for a long time afterwards."

Jazzy thought about Michael's hurt expression when she was late on their first day of making the 3D speeder. His trust was something she was just starting to earn, and now she was risking it for a party. But it was a party she'd wanted to go to ever since she could remember. In the corner of May and Sophie's room, Jazzy examined herself in the full-length mirror. Her hair, makeup, and costume were perfect. "Maybe no one will find out," she said softly.

"Maybe," May replied.

Jazzy sure hoped so.

Chapter Eight
The Big Party

At the cinema, kids vibrated with excitement.
Haley's dad had closed the entire theater just
for Haley's party. A series of giant, cardboard
cutouts of characters from the Star Wars
movies stood around the lobby. Next to a huge
Stormtrooper-turned-Jedi Finn, a life-sized
cutout of Haley grinned at Jazzy. An unsmiling
photographer posed the eager children around
various figures, snapping pictures. Haley's
mom, a taller, blonder version of Haley, handed
a brand new Star Wars Blu-ray to each child
who entered the party.

Thanking Haley's mom, Jazzy searched the

lobby for a friendly face. She wished Michael were there. He would make some silly pose with the cutouts. She smiled as she recalled him wielding a lightsaber with Snowda on the day he first started at her school.

The strawberry taste of her lipstick reminded Jazzy that she was gnawing at her bottom lip. Jazzy heard May's voice in her head, *You always chew your lip when something's wrong.*

Across the lobby, Alec was surrounded by kids. "Hey, Jazzy!" he shouted as he caught her eye.

She threaded through the crowd to where Alec perched inside an incredible TIE fighter that was built around his wheelchair. Each wheel was transformed into a giant twin ion engine, with Alec seated at the pilot's controls of the starfighter ship.

"Wow! That TIE Fighter is spectacular!" Jazzy said. Bending down, she examined the detailed hexagonal panels. "How did you make this?"

"I didn't," Alec said. "You're the one with the mad costuming skills." He laughed. "The

501st Legion built it."

"The 501st Legion?"

"They are this volunteer group that makes really high quality costumes. Some of their stuff is for kids in wheelchairs. We contacted them, and they sent me this." He sat taller in his chair as he spoke. "I get to use the costume for now, and when I outgrow my chair, I'll pass this to another kid who uses a chair this size."

"That's so nice!"

A girl squealed as she approached the TIE Fighter. "You look super, Alec!"

The girl was an exact replica of *The Force Awakens'* Maz Kanata. Each element of her Maz costume was perfect, from the wide-set goggles to the collection of friendship bracelets jangling at her wrists. Jazzy tugged on the WILDKITS wristband that Carlos had given her. She never took it off, not even when she was dressed in a costume. She wondered if anyone helped the girl make her costume. "Hi, I'm Jaz–" she started to say to the girl.

The theatre doors opened.

"Look!" The Maz girl grabbed the handles of

Alec's wheelchair. "Let's go!" she said, angling Alec through the crowd without a backward glance to Jazzy.

"Attention, everyone! The movie is starting!" Haley shouted. Kids began moving towards the entrance. The noisy kids filtered into the theater. Jazzy looked around again. Among the seats, she was relieved to find that Alec had saved her a spot right next to him in the first accessible row. "I think they are going to give everyone giant buckets of hot popcorn!" Alec said.

"Sweet!" Jazzy said. A pang of guilt ripped through her, remembering how Michael always used the word "sweet" when he was excited. With a quick shake of her head, she settled in next to Alec.

"Sorry, Jazzy." Haley stood with her hands on her hips. One of her triple Rey buns had turned renegade and a spray of blonde hair sprung sideways from her head. "That's my seat."

Jazzy inspected the velvet armrests. Had she missed some sign that the seat was reserved?

"Er, okay," she said.

Jazzy stood to move into the aisle, searching for another spot. There was an empty seat in the back row. Her cheeks burned as she climbed the stairs, the feathered train of her organza gown clutched in one hand. The lights dimmed, and the opening music soared to life. Immediately, Jazzy's mood improved. It was impossible not to lose herself in the excitement of the story! Jazzy held her breath during every tense moment and slumped with relief when the Resistance fighters triumphed.

After the credits rolled, Haley's dad stood in front of the kids. He had a thick mustache and wore jeans with a blue sweater and collared shirt peeking out at the neck.

"I hope you are all excited for the costume contest!" he boomed. "The grand prize winner and the first runner-up will join Haley and me at C2E2, where you will get to meet some of the cast members in person!" Loud clapping and cheering reverberated across the room.

Jazzy blinked as she emerged from the dimly lit theatre. During the movie, Haley's party planners had transformed the lobby into a fashion show setting. A long elevated catwalk extended the length of the room, and chairs lined the stage in three neat rows.

To Jazzy's surprise, Haley had even thought to make sure there was a ramp for Alec. But Jazzy couldn't get close enough to Alec to talk with him. A fuss of kids encircled him, with Haley smack in the middle. Extending her arm high into the air, Haley snapped selfies and made silly faces, a gold charm bracelet swinging around her wrist.

One by one, the kids had a chance to walk the catwalk and model their costumes, while a panel of judges scribbled secret scores. Someone had helped Haley smooth her triple buns back into shiny swirls. She looked just like Rey as she made her way down the runway. Greta Williams surprised everyone as a fearsome Darth Vader, with a flowing black robe and a masked helmet that even made the scary breathing noises.

When it was Jazzy's turn, her classmates oohed and ahhed as the feathers on her beautiful cape fluttered behind her. For his turn, Alec zipped up the ramp and wheeled down the catwalk. Kids started to chant, "Breakdance, breakdance!" But because of his cumbersome costume, Alec was only able to execute a few quick spins. Still, everyone cheered. Alec turned pink with pleasure. The girl in the Maz Kanata costume was the final contestant. She focused her goggles, leaned forward, and slowly peered around the room, just as Maz would do.

A real set of drums sat next to the catwalk, and Haley pounded out a drumroll for the announcement of the winners. Jazzy leaned forward. Greta Williams whooped when her name was called. The Maz girl was first runner-up.

For the rest of the party, Jazzy ate her cake, watched Haley open gifts, and picked up her personalized goody bag without saying a word. Biting her lip, she wondered how the *Star Wars* Art and Design Competition was going.

Inside her goody bag, Jazzy saw a deluxe Lego set she already owned, candy she didn't like, and a t-shirt with "I Partied with Haley" printed on it. Why had she chosen this party over the competition with Michael? If only she could go back to the beginning of the day and make a different choice. Every few minutes, Jazzy peeked at her watch, desperate for Alec's mom to come pick them up.

Chapter Nine
The Truth

A scratching noise at her bedroom door woke Jazzy early on Sunday morning. May and Sophie liked to sleep in on weekends, but Sing was ready to play and always came to Jazzy's room. Jazzy threw back the tangled covers on her bed and opened the door. Wriggling and panting, the excited dog bounded into the room.

"I couldn't sleep anyway," Jazzy said to Sing, rubbing her behind the ears. They sat together for a few moments. Then Jazzy squeezed her eyes shut. "I have to apologize to Michael, don't I?"

Just saying the words out loud made them

feel a tiny bit less awful. Sing rolled over and licked Jazzy's cheek. "I'm glad you still like me," she sighed. She only hoped Michael would still like her, too.

Jazzy walked downstairs. She stepped into the sunny kitchen where Mom and Dad sat side by side at the counter with the newspaper spread out in front of them.

"Tell us all about the big competition yesterday!" Mom said, as she poured vanilla-flavored cream into her steaming mug of coffee.

That was all it took. Mom's kind expression burst the balloon of pressure in Jazzy's chest. She erupted into heaving sobs. Once she started talking, she realized how much there was to say.

"And I just wanted to be included by Haley for once in my life! Mom, you know how hard it is that she's never asked me to one of her parties! When it finally happened, I couldn't give it up. So I lied to Michael," Jazzy finished, sniffing.

Mom sighed, and Dad frowned. There was a long silence while they seemed to be thinking about what to say. Mom rubbed her forehead.

"Jazzy, first, I want you to know that I'm glad you told us. It took a lot of courage to admit what you did." Mom's supportive words made it a little bit easier to look her parents in the eyes.

"You know, Jazzy," Mom continued, "I think that what we do with a mistake after it happens might be just as important as the mistake itself. Sometimes, it's even more important. People are usually willing to forgive you if you own up to what happened and work to repair the damage."

"I'm sorry I lied to you," Jazzy said. Dad's eyes were sad, and he said, "I know you are."

Mom stood up and walked to counter where a stack of napkins perched next to a bowl of fruit. She grabbed a few napkins off the top and handed them to Jazzy. "Sometimes telling one lie leads to telling more lies to cover for the first lie."

"Yeah," Jazzy said. "After I lied to Michael, I had to lie to you guys."

It was quiet while Jazzy mulled over what she had done.

"It's kind of like what we are learning in Ms. Weir's class," said Jazzy, "about how some people want to rewrite history. I can't undo what I did, but I can try to make it better. I'm going to tell Michael the truth first thing in the morning, but I think it will take him a while to stop being mad at me. Michael already has trouble with trusting people, and I'm supposed to be his friend."

"This is going to be very hard for Michael." Mom sat back down.

"I really blew it." Jazzy bit her lip.

The next morning, Jazzy's eyes were crusty. She hadn't slept much the night before. As she fumbled with her locker, Michael came running up to her. He lugged a large paper bag. "Jazzy!" he exclaimed. "The competition was amazing. We should find out the results in about a week. When we signed up, we decided that the notification would be mailed to your house. So check your mail like everyday."

Michael opened the bag. "The judges took pictures and videos of everyone's projects, but then we got to bring them home at the end of the day. So I brought the speeder for us to show everyone at school."

Jazzy's took a steadying breath. Before she could even open her mouth, Shanice called to Jazzy from across the hall.

"Jazzy! You left your Star Wars Blu-ray at Haley's party on Saturday."

Michael stared at Jazzy. His eyes blazed as he stepped backward. "You went to Haley's party on Saturday? You lied to me?"

"I'm sorry! This wasn't how you were supposed to find out. I was just about to tell you..."

"Right, like I'm going to believe you now!" Michael looked down at the speeder, still held in his outstretched hands. He dropped it onto the floor. A cracking sound echoed down the hall as the speeder broke into pieces. Michael stormed down the hall.

The net they had so carefully constructed for the speeder was torn, the nose had dislodged from the body, and the steering apparatus had cracked in two. Jazzy sank to her knees. One by one, she picked up the jagged pieces of the speeder and placed them into the paper bag. This was all her fault. Everything felt broken, just like the speeder.

Chapter Ten
Broken

For the next few days, Jazzy tried to catch Michael alone. But every time he saw her, he rushed in the opposite direction. In class, she passed him notes that he pretended he didn't see. She tried calling his house, but Michael's mom's voice was icy. "I'm sorry, Jazzy. He doesn't want to talk to you."

Two weeks after the night of Haley's awful party, May knocked on Jazzy's bedroom door. "You in there, kiddo?"

All Jazzy had been doing was staring at her ceiling. "Yeah?" she called out.

May peeked her head around the door. In her

hands, she clutched a large, white envelope. "This came for you."

The envelope was addressed to Jazzy Armstrong with a metallic Millennium Falcon seal and a return address of *Star Wars* Art and Design Competition.

"The results!" Jazzy tore the envelope open as May sat at the edge of Jazzy's bed.

"We won!" Jazzy whispered, reading the letter inside. "We won!" she shrieked. The pages fell from her hands as she hopped onto the bed, standing and jumping. May picked up the fallen pages.

"Wait, Jazzy." Her eyes scanned the forms that came with the letter. "It says here that only one family can visit the Skywalker Ranch."

"What?" Jazzy stopped jumping. Out of breath, she read over Sophie's shoulder. "Oh no. That means either our family goes or Michael's does."

"What's all the shouting about?" Sophie asked as she entered the room.

"Jazzy and Michael won the design competition," May's words were measured and slow. "Two hundred dollars and a trip to the

Skywalker Ranch."

"Hey! That's awesome." Sophie looked at Jazzy's slumped shoulders. "So why the face?"

"Only one family can go," May explained.

Sophie scanned the letter and attached forms. "Well, your name is on the letter, Jazzy. So, technically, our family gets to go."

"That's true," Jazzy said, biting her lip. "I mean – Michael's name isn't on this anywhere."

Sophie shrugged. "All you have to do is fill out the forms with your name and send them in. It's going to be so exciting, Jazzy! Skywalker Ranch!"

May's voice was quiet. "Most kids only dream about going there," she said.

"Yeah!" Sophie hugged Jazzy. "I'm not even a big *Star Wars* fan, but I'm stoked to see the ranch! Okay, I have to practice my cello or Mr. Kigami is going to rake me over hot coals."

The room grew quiet after Sophie left. May rubbed Jazzy's back. "I should finish my homework, Jazzy. You okay?"

"Mmmm hmmm," Jazzy stared at the papers. She hardly noticed as May slipped out of the room. Outside, it was snowing again. She sat, thinking for a long time.

At school the next day, Jazzy felt a lot lighter. She'd mailed off the forms early that morning. Near the lockers, she watched Michael's back retreat down the long hallway. Today, she wasn't going to let him ignore her. "Michael!" she called out. "Wait!"

Michael looked back at Jazzy. His face puckered, but he stopped walking.

Jazzy ran to him. "I know you're mad at me," she said. "But I wonder if you'd still be willing to help me get the new snow off the playground? I have a great idea about solving our problem!"

Michael twisted the straps of his backpack. "For Alec?"

Jazzy nodded.

"I'll help. But for Alec, not for you."

Michael's words hurt, but that wasn't important. "Thanks," she said. "I'll meet you at the playground at lunchtime?"

"Okay," Michael turned and made his way down the hall.

Jazzy took a deep breath. This had to work.

Chapter Eleven
Shovels and Apologies

By lunchtime, Jazzy had gathered ten of her classmates outside. Each held a brand new shovel. When Michael came out of the building, he stopped in his tracks. "What? Where did all of these shovels come from?" The kids were hard at work, scooping snow and clearing not only the path, but the basketball court, too!

Jazzy couldn't help it. Her smile felt so big that it practically hurt her cheeks. "We won!" she shouted. "We won the *Star Wars* Art and Design Competition!"

Michael's mouth fell open.

"I hope you're not mad, but I used the $200

in prize money to buy these shovels," Jazzy said. She handed him a large shovel with a shiny blue handle.

Michael laughed. "Sweet!"

Jazzy blew out air she didn't realize she'd been holding in. Michael was happy.

"Come on," she said.

The two children joined their classmates as they hefted snow in corners of the playground. Within twenty minutes, the whole space was as smooth as glass. The kids cheered.

"We did it!" Michael whooped along with the other kids.

Jazzy hadn't felt this good since she and Michael last worked on the speeder.

Kids poured out of the building. At first, Alec rolled out like it was any other day. Then he looked around. "Hey!" he shouted. "Wow!"

Alec wheeled across the cement surface. He looked at each of the kids who still held shovels. "Thank you, everyone!" Alec popped a wheelie. The kids clapped and laughed. Some of them dropped their shovels to join Alec in a pickup game of basketball.

Mr. Budzik walked over to Jazzy and Michael. "You kids did a nice thing here," he said. "Can you do it every time it snows?" Mr. Budzik asked.

Jazzy and Michael looked at each other. "You bet," Jazzy said. "I'll make sure of it."

"Then I'll gather up the shovels and store them in the shed. On snow days, I'll make sure the shed is unlocked so you kids can get them."

Ms. Weir came outside without a coat. "I saw through the window. You figured out what matters most. A-plus, you two. You make a great team."

"Thanks," Jazzy said.

Ms. Weir shivered. "I have to get my coat!" She ran back into the building.

"Michael?" Jazzy reached for his arm. "There's one more thing."

He turned to face her, his expression guarded. Jazzy realized he was probably preparing to hear bad news.

"Only one family is allowed to go to the Skywalker Ranch," she said. "So I wrote down your family's name."

Michael looked confused. "Wait, what?"

"Get ready for the trip of a lifetime!" Jazzy said.

Michael reached out and put a hand on Jazzy's arm. "You did that for me?"

Jazzy's beamed. She nodded and said, "I want to be a better friend."

"This is the nicest thing a friend has ever done for me," he said.

"You deserve it," Jazzy said. "Hey, do you want to see if my mom can take you, me, and Alec for hot chocolate after school today?"

"Sweet!"

Jazzy pulled off her gloves one by one. Although the weather report that morning had announced it would be a high of twenty-five degrees that day, and snow drifted down from the sky, Jazzy wasn't cold. As Alec lobbed a ball right into the basketball hoop, Jazzy thought about what mattered most to her. Being a good friend warmed her from her boots to her fingertips.

Glossary of Terms

Birth Mother – The biological mother of an adoptee.

Birth Brother – The biological brother of an adoptee.

Open Adoption – An adoption where the birth family and the adoptive family have some form of contact. This could be as simple as knowing each other's names or as involved as regular visits.

Wheelchair breakdancing – The art of breakdancing while seated in a wheelchair. One of the most famous wheelchair breakdancers is Maksim Sedakov, who is able to perform amazing feats in his wheelchair.

Foster care – Foster care is a temporary home for children who need a safe place to live when their parents or legal guardians are unable to take care of them. Their families often struggle with many difficult conditions.

If you enjoyed this book... make your voice heard!

Want to see more of Jazzy and her friends? Would you like to see more books about adoption, fostering, and diversity?

You can make it happen!

We would greatly appreciate your taking a quick minute or two to write an online review for this book. Online reviews are an extremely important tool for readers, authors, libraries and bookstores to spread the word about interesting new books. Every review counts.

Thanks and happy reading!

Other adoption-related books published by Marcinson Press:

Jazzy's Quest: Adopted and Amazing!

Awakening East: Moving our Adopted Children Back to China

Geezer Dad: How I Survived Infertility Clinics, Fatherhood Jitters, Adoption Wait Limbo, and Things That Go "Waaa" in the Night

The New Crunch-Time Guide to Parenting Language for Haitian Adoption

Ladybug Love: 100 Chinese Adoption Match Day Stories

Are You Ready to Adopt? An Adoption Insider's Look from the Other Side of the Desk

The New Crunch-Time Guide to Parenting Language for Chinese Adoption

Available through Amazon.com and by request through most major and independent bookstores.

MARCINSON PRESS